A Monk in Paradise

A Monk in Paradise

albert klassen

A Monk in Paradise

Publisher: DEE ELL PUBLISHING

ISBN: 978-1-7782809-3-1

Further information: albertklassen@icloud.com

Books by Albert Klassen

the death of the girl with the beautiful hair
looking at life from an angle
the life of lido pepperman
the church
radical madness
a monk in paradise
the abstract god
journey
never been to berlin

One

get up in the morning and have a coffee
it's better than a spot of tea
and with that let's have a piece of cake
that someone had the foresight to bake

after that let's jump in the lake
it's fantastic for heaven's sake
wakes you up and makes you strong
and you'll be happy all day long

then we get dressed and go to work
and put up with our boss who's a certified jerk
why are bosses such big assholes
who prey on us and steal our souls

it's a sunny day and you skip down the road
maybe you'll see a red horned toad
or perhaps dame Francis will give you a wave
as he secretly wishes you were in a grave

one never can tell what people are thinking
even as they spend their lives stinking
they look at you and smile
but their thoughts on you are sometimes quite vile

and so it goes as you live out your life
trying to escape the stranger with the butcher knife
who's sneaking around and plotting your death
with his evil smile and very bad breath

in the air the munchkins dance
all day long they shimmy and prance
coasting on sunbeams and zipping along
having a good time and doing no wrong

where are the witches and goblins hiding
are they in the hedges recklessly abiding
scheming to wreck havoc in our affairs
dancing in the shadows and putting on the airs

there was a woman at the well
she was strongly pulling at the bell
give me water for I thirst
if you don't I'll have you cursed

then along came a Jesus who gave her to drink
he was dressed in lavender and purple and pink
she said thank you dear Saviour I love what you wear
and thanks so much that you care

it was a moment so tender and soft
twas not something you see too oft
then the lord walked to Calvary
to do his job and set mankind free

but in the cellar the devil lurked
he sat in ashes and he smirked
what a nasty guy was he
he did not want mankind to be free

far away the orchestra played
as all the players the conductor obeyed
they played so fine like they were on fire
beside them sang an old folks choir

and still the warm winds blew
as the damsel fainted right on cue
the faeries sprinkled moondust on the lovers
as they huddled underneath the covers

secret passageways to the otherworld
in the dark the virgins twirled
hoping to be picked to conceive a god
hoping to get a celestial nod

Two

the lords of carnage beat their chests
dialling up the volume and increasing the arrests
should not the people fear their power
as they stand high up in Langdon Tower

their hero was the Führer himself
who from his past was casting a spell
and compelling the people to listen to his voice
telling them to make him their choice

in the square sat dodo the clown
as the madness swirled around the sacred town
he was crying tears of sadness as he read the news
that the pope had died because he had the blues

do we have to fight
to prove that we're right
or is it self-explanatory
that Fred killed John Dory

it's a wasteland here in dum dum county
without circumstance and without a Mountie
no one to keep the peace and keep us safe
no solace for the little midsummers night waif

Greta was eating her egg salad sandwich in the park
it was getting oh so dark
and along came a monster who bit her upon the leg
he mistook her for a wench called Meg

the jester climbed upon a rock
he climbed up the rock and took off his sock
his sock was red and blue and white and black
and his pants were made from a gunny sack

ten philosophers sitting in a tree
all of them hoping to see
an Englishman fall down from the sky
hit the earth and start to cry

there was a man called Tom Thumb
who liked to pick his smelly bum
his wife told him that he was crass
she wacked him upon his dirty ass

if you break the law you go to jail
so act lawful and eat some kale
either way you're falling from grace
and Satan will spray you with some mace

once upon a time there was nobody
it was something you could not see
nobody was there
nobody gave a care

a noise is only something if it is heard
by something like a flying bird
and as it flies it dives and swoops
and on some hapless human poops

who can measure love
who can catch the albino dove
who can tell us how to live
who can teach us how to give

he went to the dungeon because he would not rhyme
sent to the prison till the end of time
there to fester in his stench
oh baby what a stupid mensch

hold forth thy hand oh brother
and don't show it to another
for we will be friends forevermore
or at least until you become a bore

so sail on silly ship sail on
and let no one give you the con
as you slip the berth and sail far away
hoping to find a sunny day

starting is no easy task
we'd rather in misery bask
and lie in bed till ten past eight
making it to work late

then we'll join the Buddha club
lazing in a beer-filled tub
losing ourselves in a hibernation nap
and believing all that enlightenment crap

our mind will be hazy
as we get very lazy
and forget about working
watching the hot girls twerking

Three

then God rubbed his furry balls and said pray tell
who shall I throw into my new and red hot hell
I know said the angles as they danced in glee
throw in lucifer cause he smells like pee

do not said the devil as he flew into heaven
let's throw in Jesus when I count to seven
but they didn't cause he was gods son
and that wouldn't have given God any fun

she smiled at him and rubbed his face
baby you're such a basket case
but you smile so sweetly and cause me to blush
and wish me well after I flush

why do we suffer such delusion
and come to a stupid conclusion
whenever we see a fair maiden cry
whenever we see her sigh

yes indeed we do for that's a rule
did we not all learn about it in school
where we learned to lie and cheat and fart
and some of us even got smart

in Israel the flowers grow
between the tanks row on row
where Alice tends her garden and goes to smoke
a big and fat and juicy toke

three crosses stood upon a hill
a girl named Frank forget to take her pill
now she has a son and his name is John
he's thankful that it isn't Don

the rebel stood on the bleachers and sang a song
about how much he hated King Kong
nobody listened and nobody cared
except for sue as her body she bared

he was a horses ass
he was a little crass
he let out some smelly gas
so the teacher kicked him out of class

Ringo Starr thinks he's cool
and that he's not a fool
I'm a Beatle he says
and then flicks open his pez

Paul who is a dandy
stops and takes a candy
then walks down the street
hoping John again to meet

but John is gone to another land
where Larry Norman leads the band
it's where Jack the ripper's serving time
and Marvin Gay is creating a new rhyme

throw out the lifeline to the pure of heart
who are so self-righteous they won't dare to fart
we will never become a whore
oh no - we're much too pure

hey there goody two shoes how are you
can you spare a shoe or two
no I have none to spare
so please walk around bare

meanwhile back in the mansion they were counting
sheep
and making love with little bo peep
scandalous said the mistress to her class
take off your knickers and expose your ass

thine ass thine ass a penny for thine ass
oh mister why art thou so crass
enough said the judge as he slammed down his gavel
your case is starting to unravel

Sally was a girl who liked to pamper
herself even as she did scamper
across the street to the field of dreams
where her boyfriend was up to his no-good schemes

the planning did not go well
as the principle said what the hell
let's just go home early and call it a day
and try to think of another way

Four

the monster crawled out from under my bed
it stuck it's face close to my head
I tried to run with all my might
even as I was consumed with a horrible fright

they were very bad people that I saw
I would have killed them but it was against the law
so I poured exlax into their tea
and watched them poop and pee

it was disgusting I'll grant you that
but I was crazy like a bat
they drove me nuts till half insane
I wacked them senseless with my cane

it felt so good to hurt them so
I felt the pleasure blow by blow
they came from Satans ghastly lair
so the punishment I inflicted was just and fair

I drank and danced about the hall
and then I heard my master call
oh servant come and wipe my ass
as in thy face I blow some gas

oh master please not gas again
it's going to make me go insane
I'm sick and tired of all that stink
why do you act like such a dink

and so I kicked my masters face
and told him that he was a case
I quit my post and went my way
that's all I had to say

and so at long last I was free
it was the only way to be
I once was lost but now I found
myself barking like a greyhound

on top of the table I saw a beer
I grabbed it and wished everybody some cheer
let's drink this beer and eat some chips
then watch as Johnny Black does backflips

going to a dark place in your mind
a place where nobody is kind
where jackals sneer and rabbits run
and everyone is feeling like they're done

a parade of delinquents putting out the fires
tis a picture for the country squires
as they politely walk to the side
not wishing to be counted as one who had died

and where is meaning when you need her
running down the street in her red fox fur
she never looks you in the eye
but loves to eat banana cream pie

hang on to your life mister
no one else will care a pister
they'll shoot you down in a second
so different than what you reckoned

and when at the bottom of the tree you peer
on that white morning when you're so full of cheer
and find no present addressed to you
then know that you are unloved too

it will be alright in a couple of years
after a shedding of all those tears
anew then you can start to build
some love for those that you'd have killed

Five

falling from the sky into a lake
it was an unidentified object that looked like a cake
where did it come from
from where did it come

we wander as we wonder
why is there thunder
and who invented the sun
why was it all done

curious as a cat
sometimes even fat
asking questions all the time
paying not a dime

the artist cleared his throat as he painted
then his girlfriend fainted
he stopped to help her up
and put some water in a cup

lean on me if you want to
just don't kick me into the loo
cause it's nice to be wanted
it feels so vaunted

lemons are sour and yellow
the monk is quiet and mellow
the choir sang sweetly
and the couple kissed discreetly

lay it all down
you multicoloured clown
and don't shoot the king
instead give Elvis a ring

how close were they
when they lived down by the bay
every night they would kneel down and pray
to ensure tomorrow would be a nice day

Ulysses sailed away so far
he didn't even own a car
he loved sirens and beaches
but hated blood-sucking leaches

so join together and say hi
as you dream of pie in the sky
where Aphrodite cavorts with Zeus
and together they drink cauliflower juice

dance mortal dance upon this stage
take the book of life and turn the page
and see where sadness fades and glory shines
and Isabella for you pines

it's all so senseless don't you think
as we wash our ideals down the sink
in the end it's only money that is true
it's all that will mean anything to you

so save your money every day
and try not to waste it away
without it you cannot live
without it you have nothing to give

jump for joy oh daughter of Zion
what's with all those clothes you try on
is there trouble with your mind
do you suffer from words that are unkind

take a walk along the water
walk there slowly with your daughter
and thank god for the gift
even though sometimes she's miffed

Six

holy holy holy smokes
sammy's telling dirty jokes
he's a funny little guy
I wouldn't tell a lie

if you let him he'll talk all night
never let you see the light
he's a guy who knows it all
even though he's very small

a penny for your thoughts frauline queer
why don't you wipe away that sneer
are you sick of all your dirty deeds
are they interfering with your natural needs

if only all those tools weren't so cheap
they belong in a giant heap
cheaply made and dangerous to use
who should we accuse

thunderstruck in the ancient city of rome
where lots of weirdos make their home
and the nutty guy wears dresses
even as the world he blesses

when you love someone
it's time to run
not into their arms
lest you trip all of the alarms

feeling alive and full of zest
ready for your quest
to conquer the world
and have your hair curled

the funny guy said I'm gonna dare em
to have a harem
a whole house full of chicks
to give him lots of kicks

windows on the world are open for fun
everyone dancing in the sun
and playing games so strange
trying to rearrange

hanging out in outer space
and making a case
for being an intergalactic hermit
and shooting rockets without a permit

an antigravity state of mind
may not be the kind
of attitude that benefits a spacewalker
even though the astronaut was a good talker

fiddlesticks she said as she slapped him hard
you stupid old dummy card
I won't have anything to do with you
with you my friend I am through

indeed said the real estate broker
why are you such a poker
poking around here and there
finding nothing anywhere

go fishing in the deep
find a treasure to keep
then put it on a shelf to display
that you are not okay

it's a sign of the times
that people turn themselves into mimes
parroting everything they hear
and drinking oldenhauser beer

Seven

twas in 1620 that the mayflower arrived
and the spirit of that arrival has survived
a spirit of freedom and of hope
to help a persecuted people cope

and still today the downtrodden continue to arrive
seeking for a way just to survive
to a land of endless sun and Liberty
where all people can live in peace and harmony

the American Dream shines a light
in a darkened world so filled with night
where if you want to work and have a dream
you get to have milk with all the cream

1969 was a wall
everyone was on call
as bell bottoms and beads
clashed with good old fashioned deeds

painted ladies went on rampages
opening all the doors to their cages
baring much more than their soul
as the speakers blasted out some rock and roll

the status quo took a giant hit
as everyone did their bit
to open up their eyes
and quit with all the lies

words of wonder words of cheer
seems our lord is drawing near
and when he comes he'll whip thine ass
cause all thine life thou hast been crass

on the thunder clouds he will arrive
then swoop down into a dive
he will play some rock and roll
over by a grassy knoll

Angels will be dancing with the king
as with trumpets they will sing
hosanna to the lord of might
who brings the day and bans the night

wake up wake up you sleepy head
time to get up from thy bed
with the angels you must dance
as all around the pole you prance

quietly tip toe into the garden
where the jailer gives you a pardon
and forgives all your sin
then pouring you a glass of gin

it's a clear blue morning
and the natives are sending a warning
don't trespass on our land
and disrespect our band

it was our land first
even though you may thirst
for ownership and domination
and satisfaction

are there principles that matter
to people like the mad hatter
or is it do what you want
even as the weirdos taunt

it's a big world my friend
and we all want to be happy in the end
why make your neighbour mad
and his family sad

jump for joy and wear a smile
take a snack when you walk a mile
and eat pumpkin pie every day
it's sure to brighten up your way

Eight

it carried with it a lot of weight
that big old number eight
it sat at the edge of a cliff
as if it had had a tiff

seven days are in a week
and then came the end of the streak
with a lonely number at the end
and no more messages to send

one is a lonely number that's for sure
it's first so it is pure
but it has six other friends all in a row
so it never feels very low

one two three four five six seven
all those numbers go to heaven
but then you have the number eight
to go to hell that is its fate

oh woe is me it cried out loud
then went to the corner where it cowed
and sighed with a broken heart
why can't I have a part

it's tradition what can we do
but go along too
with seven days a week we're stuck
so it looks like number eight you're out of luck

there are souls that stretch like elastic
together unbroken they click
as fighting for love they disarm
and keep each other from harm

like a rocket that electrifies
even as it terrifies
she paraded down the street
moving sensually to the beat

please release all the spells
and ring all the chapel bells
cause there's trouble in the galaxie
someone suspended gravity

orange splatters of paint on the floor
lines of black on the door
a mystery guest is coming to town
they love to be known as a clown

the street party rocked my socks
the hairdresser cut her locks
the butcher cut up the meat
the teacher printed very neat

deprived of sleep she flung herself on the couch
she hit the side and said ouch
and then she drifted off to sleep
woke up in the morning when her phone said beep

at the bakery the croissants were warm
then Bob bought some and took them to his dorm
he ate them with strawberry jam
and when he finished he said - dam

the coach said keep on running
he was evil and very cunning
if you slowed down he'd slap your face
and call you a stupid basket case

fiddle dee dee dum
Betsy was playing with her gum
she put some on her chair
and even got some in her hair

and then we'll rise to sing the anthem at the beach
and then we'll listen to the preacher preach
and then we'll sing a song of sixpence full of rye
and then we'll all sit down to sigh

Nine

a return to senselessness is in the cards
so please people don't let up your guard
be vigilant and watch the door
even if you are lazy to the core

it was a triumphant march
even though the pants were filled with starch
the prisoners were then shot into the ditch
life can be such a bitch

they came at night and stole the prize
then went to the deli and had some fries
it was a motley group that did the deed
the warnings of the judge they did not heed

in a fortnight they were all in jail
the next day none of them made bail
so up on the scaffold for the hangmans noose
that's what they got for playing fast and loose

there is the night and then the dawn
then comes Mary and soon she's gone
no one can find her she went away
but she cut her hair and she's okay

as I sat in the sun I listened to the lullaby
and looked up at the sky
sweet dreams were floating
as I watched the sailers boating

casting all our cares upon the crucified
we became ourselves deified
or at least it's what we thought
as we were surprised at what we got

the pilgrims languished at the seaside
after a terrifying joyride
and then enjoyed a bottle of wine
after worshipping at the shrine

all the holy men gathered at the mouth of the cave
which had become a grave
to an old decrepit monk
who now stank like a skunk

mortality really sucks
it's then that we say ah shucks
wish we had more time
to be merry and drink the wine

but the dice are cast
and even if we fast
and do penance
we have to do the death dance

dance mortal dance
we all get at least one more chance
one more kick at the can
to increase our lifespan

the eagle spreads its wings and glides
the tanner tans his hides
the lord abides
the judge decides

let all the sunshine in to your soul
and move to the music of the rock and roll
a shimmy to the left and a shimmy to the right
find a place where it's sunny and bright

the coal miner found a way to groove
he made his body move
and the ladies thought that he was cool
and threw him into the pool

and somewhere in the universe there is hope
even as the hopeless grope
for something to hang onto
that will stop them feeling blue

Ten

can you see the white knight
does he give you a fright
and can you give up the lies
before your innocence dies

walk slowly in the park
don't go there after dark
a photograph might accost you
waiting to say boo

and can you read the writing on the wall
will you run to catch the ball
as it bounces back to your childhood
and makes you feel so good

tap your foot and smile
watch Jesus walk that lonely mile
sacrifice your sadness for some joy
as you jump and act so coy

joseph and mary went to the stable
didn't even have a table
put their baby in the manger
where it was safe from all kinds of danger

it was a heavenly nursery
a start to the end of misery
it would be a long hard road
where God would break the Devils code

demons stand around the golden globe
satan's wearing his long white robe
they sing love songs in the dark
as their minions have a picnic in the park

where oh where can we find a sliver
of that which only makes us quiver
the ancients gave up on their quest
but we continue out here in the west

there is a mule who will kick
the interaction will make you sick
as you fly through the air
as the natives stop and stare

look at the dude flying through space
wonder if he'll land on his face
and scratch it up real bad
what a fad

I looked for common ground
for a theory which was good and sound
could not mankind all agree
on something which would keep us free

why do we always have to fight
everyone thinking that they are right
and getting rude and rough
wanting all the stuff

sitting in the ivory tower
and lusting for more power
with a smirk upon our faces
as we hate on all the races

the team did cartwheels on the road
and stepped upon a horned toad
who hopped away very fast
as the fans looked on aghast

china girl drank her tea and sang her song
Bowie was dead so he couldn't sing along
but what the hell
she sang it well

have some cake and drink some gin
dig a hole and jump right in
meditate and do a dance
and dream of flying away to France

.

Eleven

an endless cacophony greets the day
as the seagulls are determined to have their say
and is it a conscious decision
to have double vision

they say that two are better than one
and two are a lot more fun
cause one is a lonely number
especially when you slumber

waking up to yourself is a drag
you feel like an old rag
if only there was someone else there
with whom to care and share

did your differing views drive you apart
or was it because you made a fart
and stunk up the entire place
such a smelly case

and now alone you lie
asking yourself why
wishing you could have them back
someone to share the lonely sack

together you could go shopping
and maybe even bar hopping
and look for rainbows in the mist
drink some beer and get real pissed

alone again it's sad to hear
as you drown your sorrows in the beer
looking for someone
so you can have some fun

to be alone it has to suck
it makes you want to say oh yuk
if only I had made it work
and not been such a nasty jerk

regret is knocking on the door
of pain it wants to give you more
until you're lying on the floor
your life a total bore

oh well you sigh
I used to fly
but now I'm feeling very low
and don't know where to go

so you call up your mother and say you're sad
in fact you're really mad
why can't I find that special one
someone that I call hon

and who wants to play the dating game
everyone seems to be all the same
they smile at you and tell you lies
until you gag and your interest dies

they ask you do you want to go to bed
and try to get into your head
but you can't be bothered it's too much work
around the corner the problems lurk

oh number one I hate you so
you never ever say ho ho ho
with you a reflection is all I see
and the only one I have is me

and so I go to bed
to rest my weary head
my feet they feel like lead
sometimes I feel I'm dead

Twelve

get up and drink a coffee tea or beer
and pipe some music to your ear
eat a muffin or a scone
and talk to someone on the phone

getting up is hard to do
especially if you have to poo
pull down your pants and let it fly
and wish your shit bye bye

the sun is shining bright
and you are quite a sight
brush your teeth and comb your hair
and learn to walk on air

who should you be today
as you sing down by the bay
and dream of faeries and of elves
who want to be themselves

choo choo says the train
everyone here is half insane
putting on an act
and acting like they're wacked

ya ya we are all nuts
as we stare at all those butts
no one has the guts
to patch up all the cuts

oh brother sister uncle aunt
why do you always say I can't
for once why don't you say I do
instead of acting like you don't have a clue

meandering along life's path
feeling the pain of someone's wrath
as you eat your donut on the bench
and dream of speaking French

bonjour Monsieur comment cava
why don't you go to a wonderful spa
and jump in a tub and have a soak
then light up with a big fat toke

make your life a fairytale
where you're not trying to make bail
read your bible and dream of God
or of someone with a very hot bod

tra la la la la la la
ra ra ra ra ra ra ra
stick a nickel in the slot
and baby don't get caught

if a copper gives you a ticket
please don't take it to the wicket
cash it in and buy a dream
and eat some cake with lots of cream

perhaps a croissant will make you smile
as you run another mile
to get off all that weight
as you get ready for your date

an apple a day
keeps the doctor away
who lives to see you in pain
and drives everyone insane

crazy people line the streets
listening to the rock bands beats
dancing up a storm
resisting the call to conform

up the paddle without a creek
everyone should be unique
why be like Monique
when you can be a total geek

Thirteen

they said oh no no no no no
there cannot be a ufo
but here it comes again
we can't all be insane

dare to defy gravity
dare to fly free
nothing pulling you down
as you glide above your town

oh how she did squeal
when she saw the alien was real
she was aghast
and ran away fast

help me help me I saw an alien in the sky
and I wasn't even high
he looked at me
as I my pants did pee

from whence did they come
where are they from
are we all dumb
why are we so numb

we dream of impossible things
but then shut down what the universe brings
it lays miracles at our feet
and we go dancing to a different beat

it's within the ether that we live
without it we have nothing to give
within and without it covers us
and sings to us when we're on the bus

so ride that magic bus forever
and never leave it ever
the driver will be with you for all time
and he can stop right on a dime

someday to the moon we all will go
who's going to say no
jump in your spaceship and fly away
you will be okay

outer space will be our land
we will conquer it with the human hand
shaping our future as we investigate
moving on from watergate

why do we doubt our ability
to increase our fertility
by taking steps to conquer space
for the future of the human race

space exploration will bring us all together
as we rise above the regions of nether
going where we've never been
looking at what's never before been seen

someday we will have ufo's too
as in some strange planet we say boo
and hover there for just a second
giving those inhabitants more than they reckoned

seems to me we've got a lot of work to do
better get busy and get off the loo
we need to be unrelenting
and get on with our inventing

watch the spacecraft rise in the air
as with courage we dare
to push the limits and cast off our fear
even as the cowards jeer

Fourteen

one day the Berlin Wall fell
what a story to tell
a divided people reunited
everyone delighted

ideology devides us all
preventing us from standing tall
we lose the magic of humanity
to the winds of calamity

hitler brought out the devil
he played us like a fiddle
as divided we turned on each other
and killed our neighbours mother

the nightmare cut us to the bone
as many hearts turned to stone
the killing reached a fever pitch
as life became a bitch

I am what I am - so god said
then he went to bed
where did God go
all I see is snow

abandoned to the wolves of war
bedevilled to the core
the refugees are sick and tired
against them the world conspired

and hidden in the mists of time
are all those statements that have no rhyme
not even reason supports their claims
as we admire those fetching dames

not everyone wants to go to heaven
not everyone likes the number seven
some people like it hot not cold
and some are happy to be old

the colour red is hot as hell
a cardinal must ring the bell
who is the greatest dope
I think it is the pope

he wears his fancy dresses to the ball
over everything he casts a pall
his fancy hats are all the rage
as he stalks about in his ecclesiastical cage

some people think that they're so cool
but mostly they are someone's fool
they turn their ball caps on their heads
they must be off their meds

see the jerk prance about
see him as he has to shout
see him as he tries to sing
see him try to be a king

the stained glass windows in the church
are better than a piece of birch
there are hymn books in the pews
people sit there and drink their booze

oh to be happy and oh to be drunk
and to smell just like a skunk
shifting sands a warning be
that everything is not for free

come on batter hit the ball
before the umpire makes his call
and it's strike three and you are out
then off to the dugout to cry and pout

Fifteen

have you seen the first hotrod ever made
it went so fast even in the shade
it was the old tin Lizzy
and it made us all dizzy

a soldier of fortune died on the beach
it was the capital that he wanted to reach
but a bullet put an end to that
and a local stole his hat

war is a capitalistic adventure
that necessitates raising a debenture
it's takes money to fight
to prove that you are right

a Chevy or a Ford
the engine roared
faster and faster they go
more and more they know

watch out for the riders out in the storm
let out from their dorm
to find excitement on the open road
and carry the load

they have a plan
to bring a bike to Stan
so he can get strong
and ride along

the Beatles picked strawberries
and ate raspberries
and had blueberries on toast
down at the coast

fred painted rabbits at the school
while sitting on a red bar stool
he was wearing a black wig
and his students were dancing a jig

but over at the courthouse the judge was mad
at the prisoner because he was bad
some people will not obey
and so a penalty they have to pay

Jack be nimble jack be quick
Jack quit being such a dick
eat your grits and toe the line
otherwise you'll get a massive fine

some people like to be nice
others like to roll the dice
and cheat and lie and steal
and make a crooked deal

isn't life a bitch
why are some so rich
some become a whore
while others end up poor

why do a few have so much fame
shouldn't we all be the same
and why do some have royal blood
while the rest do cartwheels in the mud

the most honourable dufus Jce
is really a most stupid schmoe
he wears a robe and smokes h_s pipe
expecting his aides his ass to wipe

everyone has different hair
life can be so unfair
some are blonde and some are bald
some by silly names are called

magnificent and great is the Eiffel Tower
in its shadow we all cower
we dream of greatness and of power
and having a wonderful hot shower

Sixteen

romantically he was devastated when she bid him
adieu
and told him that hanging out with him she could no
longer do
his heart was broken - split in two
because it was only her that he wanted to woo

love a symbol of our infatuation is
as we drop all else to focus on the love biz
all normalcy goes out the window
as we turn into some kind of weirdo

the arrows are shot out by Cupid
and then we become some form of stupid
walking around like a zombie
reciting Coleridge Pope and Gandhi

the queen of love says hush
and those involved turn to mush
their feelings on fire
as they become a frequent flier

way up in the sky they fly
so very high
soaring like birds in space
and wearing flowers and lace

listen to the Snow White dove
hearken to a thing called love
it rips your heart
and tears you apart

then shall they come from the east
and fill the granaries with yeast
a leaven for the the bread that they shall bake
and also buns and tarts and a layered cake

everyone will gather for a feast
to celebrate the coming of the Crimson beast
they'll snack on caviar and pork
and call each other names like dork

there's only senselessness in love
as feelings come to push and shove
they all bewildered run around
heaping their lovecalls on a mound

oh my I cherish thee
and my love I adore your feelings for me
I also feel the same for thee
but hold on I've got to pee

they go to sleep and dream of each other
they have no thoughts for any other
when they're apart they pine and pine
and don't feel very fine

love is a many splendoured thing
it makes all the bells and whistles ring
running there and running here
running down the street with a beer

oh drink of love my love struck friend
drink slowly for there is no end
you drink and drink but are never full
love has got a lot of pull

but you're stuck at the crossroads
when love ends and the world explodes
what used to be real and mattered
is now altogether shattered

then lie in the hammock and nurse your pain
pray to god you don't go insane
and drink some tea and say a prayer
and try hard not to care

Seventeen

alone without the music of the band
the man walked across the windswept land
he saw a million faces
and he felt yesterday's traces

it was a land of complicated themes
everywhere there were memes
tributes to the antics of the brave
who fought to stay out of the grave

lust for living was the cry
hurt sometimes was the sigh
where monsters and minstrels appeared
and things got a little weird

across fields and over bridges
cross the mountains and between the ridges
he made his lonely way
under a sky sometimes so grey

he searched to find himself
putting his ego on a shelf
and even as he was so agile
he was also very fragile

the road was sometimes rough
and he felt that he'd had enough
he didn't like it one bit
and wanted so badly to quit

there were places where the people taunted
others which he felt were haunted
some tried to steal his socks
others just threw rocks

oh god our help in ages past he prayed
thy words I have not obeyed
but even so I look to thee
to show me what I should be

sometimes the darkness got too dark
and the emptiness got so stark
that he lay down on the ground and cried
and felt like he had died

the world was arrayed against him
even the light was getting dim
in his confusion he did grope
as little by little he gave up hope

and just when all seemed lost
and his soul was cold like frost
a hand reached down
and wiped away his frown

and up he rose again
brushing off his pain
thankful for another sign
on his journey walking the line

and as he walked he saw the sorrow
that was many a folks tomorrow
and he wished that he could lend a hand
even as he walked the land

no one the voices heeded
as they from the byways pleaded
sitting like a bum
asking for a crumb

it was a heartless land that he walked
it was a sorrowful land that he stalked
where even with the laughter and the music
many were so feeble and so sick

and so the man stopped talking
but he kept on walking
looking past all that was uncouth
searching for the truth

Eighteen

down the zip line went the stranger
it felt like he was in danger
but he zipped down a strong line
so he was totally fine

appearances can be deceiving
and sometimes we seem to be receiving
some bad advice from people who smile
when in fact it's really not so vile

so buy a guitar and form a band
get some gigs and travel the land
play your music and party on
enjoy your life before you're gone

grab a beer and get real drunk
don't sit around like a docile monk
explore your options and run around nude
get in the mood and try to get screwed

in the convent the nuns prayed and fasted
and then they let loose and got blasted
there's a time to pray and a time to say
let's drink all our troubles away

the painter huddled over his easel
to paint a weasel
he was in a trance
and even did a dance

in the long run it is what it is
you got to take care of your biz
and try to save some money
and find a good honey

buy a good and strong bed
do it before you are dead
cause then a good coffin is what your need
but for now just go and smoke some weed

in the sweet by and by
we will all be high
and meet God who will give us a hand
and welcome us to his wonderful land

no one will ever go to hell
even if they were the farmer in the dell
who murdered all the cows in the barn
and ended it all by saying darn

regrets hammer at our self-worth
as we ourselves curse
but we can't change the past
we must move on if we want to last

from our mistakes we have to learn
otherwise our stomachs will always churn
let's not be nervous annies
always fumbling with our fannies

we must admit when we are wrong
otherwise we can't be strong
and in our dealings let's not be derelict
we have to show respect

life is a bugger sometimes and brings us to our knees
but if we trust each other we'll sail through like a
breeze
let's help the fallen the weak and the sick
and never act like a stupid dick

some like cloth and some like leather
but we all need to work together
we are a family here on earth
we need to be happy and filled with mirth

Nineteen

the orchestra played as one in the park
they played there long after dark
at the front the old ladies danced
at the back the old men farted and pranced

in the prisons the prisoners are sad
condemned to a life of not being glad
some big mistakes were made
now they live in the shade

you'd think we had a better way
to deal with those who've gone astray
justice is a heavy load
to carry on a bumpy road

for the criminals we have jeers
but from their mothers there are tears
broken lives are never sweet
to be sentenced is not a treat

but evil lurks among us
and sneaks up on the bus
then very deliberately
they wack us unexpectedly

and so it goes
no one gets a rose
sometimes we all smell bad
and make each other sad

it really gave us a fright
watching the monster attack a human right
grabbing it he gave it a bite
it was a horrible sight

the floor was red with blood
it was a crimson flood
violence is never a pretty sight
it's always wrong not right

the blade descended upon the poor man's neck
as he mumbled what the heck
and then his head rolled on the floor
and then continued out the door

our lust for death is morbid and dark
even as our nakedness is beautiful and stark
our innocence we traded in for fun
as we began to love the gun

we sail on a sea of angst and shame
on righteousness we lay no claim
but munch serenely on our sins
and throw our values in the bin

enslaved we beat our chests in pride
our indiscretions we try to hide
our protestations are hollow and false
our courage is gone - we have no balls

the old man shuffles down the street
he's all alone - no one to meet
his mistress lied and then she cried
his friends they all have died

he remembers when life was finer
as he sits down at the diner
and dreams of all the days gone by
and let's out an anguished sign

the clouds move in and the sky is grey
the ships sail slowly into the bay
at the old saloon the band begins
and God again forgives our sins

Twenty

a dozen roses for you mam
why thank you mr. sam
from whence have you come
are you a little dumb

when you live inside a hole
then you must adopt a role
so that you can cope
and have a little hope

where are all the dreamers
perhaps cavorting with the schemers
making plans to rule the world
with their egos all unfurled

watch out for the witches in trees
as they make holy honey from their bees
they gather round the caldron in the woods
and sell Satans children all their goods

if you want to rule
then you have to go to school
and please don't be so snide
swallow your foolish pride

in the law of the lord do you delight
on it you must meditate day and night
the precepts of the lord are just and right
altogether perfect and bringing in the light

like a drunken sailer some do lurch
backsliders who do not go to church
grab your bible and repent
before you die and your life is spent

religion is the curse that makes us great
in many ways it opened up the gate
that allowed mankind to move ahead
inventing a place to go when we are dead

heaven is a place that's very nice
there you will not find rats or mice
gates are made of pearls and the streets of gold
and nobody gets sick or becomes old

in heaven we will see all those who've died
all those loved one for whom we cried
we'll hug and kiss them with much zeal
from all our sickness we will heal

be wary of those that curse
or carry a big black purse
all they want is money
and to eat good honey

sing a song you foolish clown
sow your seed about the town
make the old girls laugh and cry
they will sigh when you say bye bye

and in the pub the sailers dance
with the harlots they do prance
then they go up to the room
and all we hear is zoom zoom zoom

hot crust buns for sale at the store
shopping can be such a bore
then we go back home and eat
put on the music and listen to the beat

restore thy soul of daughter of the east
come to the table and let's have a feast
with our lord we'll break the bread
and then it's off to bed

Twenty-One

the diplomatic bear tapped the lion on the shoulder
excuse me sir could you please move that boulder
yes indeed my friend said the lion
and by the way my name is Brian

so he moved the boulder and the bear said thanks
and added my name is hanks
and with that they went on their way
on that bright and sunny day

people can get along if they try
no reason to sit around and cry
and throw temper tantrums all the time
it's such a crime

brick by brick they built the road
beside it sat a funny old toad
who croaked the day away
and otherwise had nothing else to say

over hill and dale
the farmer rode the rail
and sang a happy song
even though the trip was long

she said I want this room to be rearranged
he said you must be deranged
she said don't live in fear of change
he said my dear I think you're strange

and so the river flows
it may be strange but anything goes
let's make things nice and fresh
who cares if they mesh

a mismatch is what we like
mix a Charlie with a Mike
see them argue see them fight
as they wonder what is right

everyone wants their own way
no one wants to acquiesce and obey
give me this and give me that
and please don't act just like a rat

who will to the top rise
and win the greatest prize
with an earring in their nose
and in their ass a rubber hose

to the battlefield we go
to see the horses in the snow
as the arrows fly about
and the men together shout

in the hall the women gather
on the toast the jam they slather
there they talk of lust and power
and how to demolish the ancient tower

old King Cole was a merry old soul
who loved to listen to his rock and roll
he treated all his subjects just like dirt
as with the women he loved to flirt

but then they kicked him off his throne
and threw him a doggy bone
and now he shuffles down the street
begging alms from those he doth meet

life can change fast on a dime
once day you're cool and then you're slime
who's to say what tomorrow will bring
maybe in your nose a ring

Twenty-Two

ten lousy sinners sitting in a tree
expecting the lord to set them free
sitting there in panties and lace
waiting for some amazing grace

and how sweet that grace would be
and all of it pretty and free
sent down from God
who gave those sinners the nod

they had done some ghastly deeds
like bobbing for apples and wearing beads
their lies were on the telephone wire
their lust like a funeral pyre

nasty little creatures they
eating their curds and whey
hurling insults on all the saints
and laughing at all the complaints

these ten were all earmarked for hell
the demons were ringing the bell
their sins their souls had seared
among the people they were feared

so why would God choose to set them free
he should have cut them at the knee
and sent them quickly to their graves
those bad and despicable knaves

but God is love not hate
and is willing to change the fate
of guilty sinners condemned to the fire
and put them in heavens holy choir

the world has gone astray
they've all gone their own way
but God sent Christ to save us all
if only we would head the call

we love to swim in our earthly slime
rebelling against God and committing the crime
of turning our hearts away from him
and turning the light to dim

a perilous journey we make on earth
of dangerous places there is no dearth
but if we only trust in the son
our salvation will be done

and so even these very bad ten
had their moment of zen
where they recognized that they had done wrong
and didn't have long

for soon they would stand at the judgement seat
and dance to the tune of heavens beat
where they would have to say why
they lived such an unholy lie

but if they made a sincere confession
they would be forgiven of all their transgression
and they could live in heaven forever
and go to hell never

oh hallelujah all praise to the king
the ten were saved and heaven did ring
with shouts of joy and anthems of hope
and God sent a cable down to the pope

and so they cherish gods amazing grace
even as they sit in panties and lace
with smiles on their faces and joy in their hearts
and their excitement off the charts

Twenty-Three

she had a face that was fake
it looked dumb for goodness sake
why do that to yourself
put your ego on a shelf

we want to be what we are not
and tie our tummies in a knot
why do we dare
so much to care

do you want to be the main attraction
just for the reaction
as people worship at your feet
and think that you are sweet

who wants to be real
who wants to squeal
who wants to be a heel
who wants to kneel

rise oh desperate lunatic
quit acting like such a pompous dick
eat some cake and drink the wine
in the end you will be fine

the goblin gobbled goobers in the tent
his eyes were tired and he was spent
a thousand prayers he prayed that day
so he could find a better way

but he didn't find a way
and so he languished by the bay
eating chips and drinking beer
and acting very queer

does anyone know the way to Penner palace
in it lives a girl named Alice
she does cartwheels down the stairs
and flips if anyone her dares

pretty pretty necklaces of pearls
hanging round the necks of all the girls
who stand together on the steps of England's church
trying to find answers to their search

we search for love and we search for truth
even as we also run from the uncouth
the habits of some people make us mad
the dilemmas of others make us sad

pay a shilling for a pound of flesh
cover up your naked body with some mesh
sell your soul to please your mind
break the law and get into a bind

a problem a day keeps peace away
as you keep on cursing all the livelong day
will there never be an answer
for the crazy night dancer

in the club the women are hissing
while outside the men are pissing
competition for a mate
brings out all the hate

the fence was red and white
it was quite a sight
at the back the flowers grew
in the house they ate some stew

a coffee with your cake
serve it hot for goodness sake
your guests will very happy be
you will surely see

Twenty-Four

a blank page stares at you
and what do you do
go out for a smoke
or a toke

put off writing because it's hard
and go eat some Swiss chard
or some chips
with some nice dips

we want to write good stuff
but wanting is not good enough
we have to make marks on paper
and not go on a caper

the situation is dire
so go sing in a choir
and don't act so dumb
go wipe your bum

the birdies sing in the treetops
they sound almost as good as the inkspots
let the song envelope you
and then listen to the doves as they coo

they like to flick their bick
they like to talk real slick
they like to fake they're sick
they like to give their cigarettes a flick

who are they
and do they pray
are they in disarray
and are they okay

no one knows
even as the heart glows
and the river flows
as we write some prose

and so we write
in spite
of not being that bright
or a source of light

oh we think that we are smart
and we love to throw a dart
at those who dare to fart
and then we throw them in a cart

yes my friend nonsense is everywhere
you can find it if you dare
you can see it if you care
as for wisdom- she is rare

many a maiden has been smitten
about it books have been written
I read about it in an ancient fable
as I sat upon my table

the philosopher wondered about life
even as he took a knife
uttered a boast
and buttered his toast

we see what we want to see
we pee where we want to pee
we be what we want to be
we knee where we want to knee

we start life as a blank page
and over time we accumulate rage
then hopefully we mellow out
and don't continue to scream and shout

Twenty-Five

the ball went up and then it came down
it made me frown
stay up you crazy ball
why do you fall

an apple fell on Newtons head
good thing he wasn't dead
he lived to try to find out
what gravity's all about

the earth stays in revolution around the sun
the moon goes round the earth and it's never done
what the heck is going on
I think my mind is gone

Einstein thought it worked a certain way
there were scientific laws to obey
he talked of time and the fabric of space
and theoretically he made a case

we understand why some people have depravity
but we don't know what causes gravity
I wish I wasn't such a mental klutz
because this problem is driving me nuts

I put up my hand and asked the teacher
what do you know about the ether
that invisible blanket that covers us all
whose particles are infinitesimally small

no one wants to say that the ether is real
but I'm a believer cause that's how I feel
I think our scientists are a little dense
cause without the ether things just don't make sense

with gravity there is an attraction
it's a very physical reaction
as forces we don't understand engage in a transaction
that is much more than just an abstraction

we ponder and think
even as we stink
up the world with our thought
as some of our theories with nonsense are fraught

we need to rethink the things that we know
maybe we're wrong and we really blow
why are scientists such great big jerks
who think they know how everything works

we far too easily make up our mind
and put ourselves in a free falling bind
it's time to reassess and rethink
and stop being a great big dink

fabric of space and space time is bogus
we really need to start to focus
and get away from all that theoretical bunk
which is just so much ridiculous junk

we need to get on an even keel
and see that the ether is real
how else could gravity work
grab a brain and learn to twerk

let go of all that falsehood
discard the mantle of sainthood
throw on some spice
and try to be nice

pick up a rusty trombone
forget about being a clone
don't go insane
grab a brain

Twenty-Six

at the seashore with the seashells
the grim reaper ringing the bells
come home oh children come
to where you came from

everyone runs away in fear
leaving all their snacks and beer
no one wants to heed the call
they'd rather go shopping at the mall

let's go to the store and take a look
maybe we will buy a book
and read a bit and get real smart
at the very least it'll be a start

then we'll fly to London to see the queen
who knows what knowledge we will glean
she's a very ancient gal
perhaps she will be our pal

Johnny led a life of leisure
then one day he had a seizure
now he sits in his chair
and combs his hair

we writhe today in shackles of hate
destruction and chaos becomes our fate
as lashing out we clash
our adversaries we bash

our opinions rise like Giants in the mist
with each word we get more pissed
it's only us that can be right
and everyone is willing to have a fight

the preacher gave his peeps a warning
do not eat pizza in the morning
instead concentrate on your career
and have a scone and a glass of beer

why is the building square
and why did the architect dare
make it so ugly and bad
it looks so sad

we sacrifice our morals for fame
everyone playing the game
so many pricks
without any ethics

the player drained the ball into the basket
over on fifth they built a golden casket
a rich man had died
but nobody cried

it was a breakaway and into the net went the puck
the coach commented on how it took luck
luck does play its part
it can give you a start

green green grass needs to be mowed
a broken down car needs to be towed
the garden needs to get howed
the river flowed

fly little bird fly
way up in the sky
fly so high
no need to cry

she painted her toenails red
and then she went to bed
and dreamed of monsters and a green haired ghost
then got up and made some toast

Twenty-Seven

way back in time they painted in caves
and acted like barbaric knaves
hunting for animals to stay alive
it was serious and no time for jive

the Romans were a big deal
they had a lot of zeal
organized and vicious they were
strong like a big old fir

later on we had the Industrial Age
mankind really turned the page
we made a lot of real cool stuff
and never had enough

now we got the computer and the Internet
it's putting us in a lot of debt
we mortgage our lives to get ahead
and make sure our dreams don't go dead

we dribble and run and fall as we live
the question is how much will we give
stay away from a life of vice
go to bed and turn on a divice

the witches gather and cast a spell
as the vicar goes upstairs to ring the bell
calling all people to worship the king
listen to the bells as they ring

oh Christmas tree how lovely you look
I saw an illustration of thee in a book
and it made me happy as could be
it was really something to see

have you ever won an award
have you ever used a sword
and cut someone and drew the blood
then fought with him in the cold wet mud

Santa rides across the heavens with his sleigh
happy and jolly he rushes on his way
with his reindeer pulling him along
all of them so sleek and strong

the kids are waiting for their presents
wondering about all the contents
excitement fills the air
the Angels stare

the weather may be cold
and your coat may be old
and your shoes may have holes
and the devil's stealing souls

the whole thing seemed so div_ne
as the queen poured the wine
so that the workers could have a sip
before she hit them with her whip

work for the night is coming
listen to the werewolves humming
they're preparing for a night of slaughter
better hang on to your daughter

raspberry New York cream cheese cake
it's the very best that one can make
it's so very very yummy
we just love it in our tummy

he built a big red barn
to keep his animals out of harm
we all need protection
even as we clamour for affection

Twenty-Eight

the blinding flash of brilliance shook the crowd
a thundering crash that was so loud
it made the rafters shake with fear
as everything remained unclear

how can you know the truth my friend
will you remain convicted to the end
can you find your very own lane
and true to yourself remain

at the front of the class stood the teacher
and taught a lesson to the preacher
who being lost in a daydream looked confused
as if he had been accused

she dreamed of being a booker
instead she became a hooker
taking her panties off
and making her Johnnies cough

who's got the balls to take the gamble
up the alley to amble
and challenge the leader of the pack
to see if the facade you can crack

so much talent in the pool
so many dummies in the school
so many men who act the fool
so many who become a tool

sleep not on beds of gullibility my friend
or else that misplaced faith will be your end
believe only a tenth of what you hear
and drown the rest out in a beer

all around on telephone wires
I see all kinds of liars
they think that they're getting higher
but really their pants are all on fire

look at willy as he dances a jig
telling us his fish was oh so big
we are so impressed
we are so depressed

why run around so frilly
trying hard not to look silly
admit that you are strange
and feel at home out on the range

it was her intention to build a house
but her husband was a louse
he took her money and ran away
now she's stuck down by the bay

it's where the watermelons grow
back to your home you dare not go
for if you do your mother will say
don't fret everything will be okay

why worry when you can fret
about flying in a jet
as you dream of smashing
while your plane is crashing

all those smiling faces
with hidden traces
of yesterday's adventures
when they got new dentures

it all feels so yummy
when you are a dummy
and never open up your eyes
to see the many brazen lies

Twenty-Nine

I know it's only Rock and roll
but it's taking a toll
on my ears
as I shed tears

Handel and McCartney are hip
they both let their music rip
one is alive and one is dead
but they all got in my head

messiah or live and let die
for which one do you cry
music makes us live
it has so much to give

and who wants the world to rule
will you change the rules at school
making the teacher look the fool
wrecking havoc with another tool

the conductors had a spat
over what kind of hat
that they should wear
as if they should even care

crumpets with tea
who would you be
would you rather coffee
what will you see

if the president was a snake
what kind of a leader would he make
and would he leave reason
just to commit treason

a commitment to be a nun
takes more time than baking a bun
it's a lonely life of solitude
and a promise never to get screwed

free as a bird
free to drop a turd
upon a persons head
and then go to bed

silly silly pumpkin eater
was not a wife beater
but he insulted her just the same
she hit him and now he's lame

edelweiss where have you gone
did I do you wrong
I saw you at the fountain
up on the mountain

how do you know
that you will reap what you sow
is it karma or is it fate
leave your diploma at the gate

who gets in and who stays out
who will cry and pout
we want acceptance
and hate rejectance

sorry this part is wrong
but whatever let's get along
and drink our smoothies in the rain
together as we go insane

everyone is a nutcase
everyone is in last place
everyone owns the first base
everyone is a basket case

Thirty

thou shalt not utter insults in order to provoke
some the fires of passion love to stoke
with unkind words that tear apart
indicative of an evil heart

sticks and stones may my bones break
but words will always ruin the cake
be careful what you say
to say bad things is not okay

why say what's on your mind
if it's heartless and unkind
try to be circumspect and wise
and serve some kindness with your fries

honest observations when they're unkind
puts your victims in a bind
and makes them feel like shit
try to think a bit

it happens when people are bored
they use their tongue just like sword
and pierce others with their cutting talk
tripping them up as they try to walk

when people have too much money
their words have far less honey
and they think that they're all that and more
getting rotten to the core

it can be a curse to be rich
cause then you turn into a bitch
expecting others to kiss your ass
and acting very vain and crass

the rich man lived in his castle in the sky
every day he smoked his money and got high
he frowned upon those who were poor
and turned his girlfriend into a whore

abuse is masked as someone's right
oh baby what a fright
take the abuser and hang them in the night
that will surely turn on a light

how can anyone be better
and make someone else their debtor
it's a fundamental human flaw
should be against the law

we want to climb the tower
so we can have more power
and become lords in our own right
and win the fight

competition breeds contempt
and we become unkempt
as we fight against our peers
subjecting them to our fears

we'll never be whole
if money is our goal
our system it doth suck
cause it demands others we fuck

we start life nursing
and end up cursing
from innocence to sophisticated trash
only happy if we find someone to bash

oh my dear you have a lovely heel
are you happy on this spinning wheel
where at others we laugh and scoff
and once you're on you can't get off

Thirty-One

it was not the case
that she would make it to first base
the umpire said out
and she began to pout

a little bird sat on our railing
even as I watched the boats a-sailing
out to sea they went
the money was all spent

over at the pub the painter was painting
inside a lady was fainting
and Jack was still nimble
sat there sucking on a thimble

down in the cellar there were candlesticks burning
at the church the butter was churning
can you see the rain falling
can you hear the vicar calling

come to Jesus friends and lovers
come out from underneath the covers
the lamb of god went through a lot of pain
when on the cross for us he was slain

if you accept him you are in
forgiven will be all your sin
you will feel the power of his love
and you will see the Snow White dove

it will fly around you as you pray
as you promise to trust and obey
bending your will to please the lord
as with Satan you cut the cord

hit that ball and let it fly
up into the stands so high
you used to be a gomer
until you hit that homer

there was a prophet named Amos
who became very famous
he called out the Jews for all their bad deeds
trying to get them to plant some good seeds

you reap what you sow
that's what we know
so plant some good stuff
or it's going to get rough

John sat down at the bar
he didn't see the Morningstar
he was living in isolation
didn't know he needed salvation

in the coming apocalypse the angel will plant some
corn
and then a beast will blow his horn
and Babylon will be destroyed
the demons will be annoyed

then booming over the intercom will be a voice
who will ask everyone to make a choice
either you choose the lord of hosts
or he'll turn you into a bunch of ghosts

the demons faces are contorted
as the truth they have distorted
they want you to do bad things
and reap the pain it brings

it was a double play at second
not something that was reckoned
the umpire gave a shout
and two players they were out

Thirty-Two

there was a crow who loved to laugh
he asked people for their autograph
a little strange twas he
it was something to see

life is filled with peculiarities
there are some real rarities
some are bakers
and others are rule breakers

do you like to sit inside your box
and never eat salmon and lox
loving your beef and brandy stew
and your macaroni too

some like them tall
some like them small
some like to dance a jig
others like to eat a pig

there are some who don't like meat
it's something that they just 'won't eat
and that's okay in fact it's alright
it's even out of sight

everyone has their own way
that they like to play
they all should have their say
on how they live their day

I hate to admit it
but I don't like a bigot
what makes them think that they are right
and all the rest are not as bright

we all bring something to the table
isn't that right dear auntie Mable
we all equal should be
and roam around proud and free

remember what we learned in school
to practise the golden rule
treat others as you would yourself
and put your ego on a shelf

just because you wear a fancy hat
don't mean you're a cool cat
that high roller we call the pope
is nothing but a dope

the pope has the biggest mouth around
he's always standing on his mound
telling us what we should think
and also what we drink

he just can't stop all his talking
why not shut up and keep walking
we're not interested in all your crap
so shut your great big trap

a messenger of God he's not
he's nothing but a mouthy snot
everywhere he sticks his nose
oh he's such a doz

we're tired of people who smell like poo
and always tell us what to do
why don't they just go away
and have nothing more to say

the phone rang
the singer sang
the gambler said dang
and his name was wang

Thirty-Three

to flirt with Molly
is always a folly
and she doesn't care
what you wear

some want to impress
instead they depress
cause it's all been arranged
that we're all deranged

out of our mind
and not even kind
just a shipload of boozers
and big time losers

but the guitar player is strumming
and your lady is humming
the evening is late
and you open up the gate

she is beautiful tonight
as you hold her tight
on a cold November night
and kiss her face that beckons in the moonlight

together you are one
intertwined lovers under the sun
completely surrendered to her heart
eternally committed never to part

the consequence of syncopated thought
is a devaluation of things that you bought
so just declare all your goods at the border
or answer to law and order

marriage is not an answer to insecurity
it won't help you with your inferiority
complex which will only get worse
as you feel the curse

invent a character you can live with
something from a myth
be what you want to be
not what you already see

you are what you wear
so try not to scare
don't be a fool
attempt to be cool

oh no the lover was jilted
and the flowers were wilted
and then did the tears flow
where did love go

love never goes away
but simply looks for a sunny day
and then it comes alive
and dances to the jive

are you fanning the flames
as you paddle down the River Thames
hoping to catch a glimpse of the queen
where she's never before been seen

why look for love where it does not thrive
in some old hut or dive
find her by a river or a stream
and live the dream

love will not stop caring
even when the sirens are blaring
and Suzy biscuits of stone doth make
instead of peanut butter cake

Thirty-Four

open up the covers and take a look
inside the very scary book
where dragons eat people and witches cast spells
and monsters climb the belfry to ring the bells

the writer is drowning in a sea of misery
as he tries to unravel a mystery
throwing his pen across the room
he settles down in an aura of gloom

it's time to pour a glass of wine
maybe then things will go fine
it's such a fight
as he thinks of things to write

who knew that life could be so tough
who knew that writing could be so rough
he puts a pistol to his head
and then eats a croissant instead

why did it take so much education
to work at this vocational
better to have been a baker
or a hat maker

he climbs into bed and goes to sleep
and doesn't make a peep
for many hours
and then wakes and smells some flowers

does he have word saturation
where is his inspiration
his talent has gone and left him in the lurch
better he go to church

down on his knees he goes
and prays even as he stubs his toes
and cries out in anguish and in pain
as his focus begins to wane

he has to take a trip
in lieu of a whip
maybe a new sight
will give his creativity a fright

and scare him back into line
sending him deep into his mine
where ideas form and demons sing
and new words to the surface bring

we pray to you oh lord of the scribes
we offer up our finest bribes
oh help us in our hours of need
then we will honour you indeed

leave us not in creative poverty stricken
but our failing limbs do quicken
inject some tonic into our brain
but not so much that we go insane

and so the writer ambles back
and tries to get on track
dispensing words across the page
as if he was a wise old sage

he can't hold back his minds on fire
he's pulled himself up from the mire
his words they flow like a raging stream
he's all caught up in his literary dream

it seems to be you have to fight
if you intend a book to write
words are stubborn and want to be free
in a sentence they do not want to be

Thirty-Five

the architect believed in absurd design
it was a sign
of his radical outlook
and his willingness to not go by the book

the status quo is bedrock
it's under key and lock
but the rebels insist on turbulence
as they defy permanence

the shape is just fine
go drink your wine
quit complaining about boredom
and go lick a big bum

we need change is the cry
and the echo asks why
only for its sake
it seems so fake

Picasso took a side street
he wanted to meet
someone interesting and vain
outside his lane

and so he went from muse to muse
looking to light a fuse
to explode his art
and satisfy his heart

we look in the garbage for rubbish
for something we can publish
a bottle or a can
or an electrical fan

she whipped him in his bed
he would rather have had sex instead
but he had been a bad boy
and had been acting far too coy

so she tied him up when he was asleep
he didn't make a peep
and then she let him have it
he woke up and said oh shit

two days later he finally was free
in his bed he had to pee
in his bed he had to poop
like a chicken in a chicken coop

build a wall inside your house
it will keep out the little mouse
then you will be warm and cozy
and your life will be so rosy

can you imagine the faces
if they said baseball must have five bases
it would have no support
they would have to go to court

we want things to stay the same
it's upsetting to change the game
to what we know we cling
that's how we swing

what's in fashion today
tomorrow could go away
then your clothes will not be cool
and you'll be thought of as a fool

she wore a white dress to the ball
which was held in the city mall
there she danced with the scribes and Pharasees
and exposed all their lies and heresies

Thirty-Six

at the bar the patrons drank
in the bathroom they stank
minds aflame with fantasy
what a way to be

the trip to the coast was a delight
there was so much light
the sun seemed to shine brighter
and everything seemed whiter

as the artist spread paint on the canvas
she got more anxious
she did not feel
that it was real

art is an imaginary journey
or so it seems to be
where does it go
no one seems to know

even a detective
can't figure out the perspective
is it an alien state of mind
that we find

perhaps our intuitive approaches are wrong
and our esoteric intuition too strong
what does it mean
and where have we been

are we repulsed by reality
put off by the nonsensibility
of subconscious influences that
make us look fat

forms are interacting
with relationships detracting
as rich and intersecting visual compositions
assume contradictory positions

violent brush stokes blend
with rigid elements that end
in an imaginary land
where plays a dishevelled folk band

whose bass player is playing in the wrong key
and the singer is wanting to be
free and wild
like a child

in the corner sits a bohemian
his hair in the proverbial bun
mixing an elixir of negative and positive space
disengaged from the human race

the structural qualities are fighting
with darkness and lighting
trying to find their voice
and a space that is choice

we manipulate optical effects
to identify where truth intersects
and then categorize our assumptions
in terms of philosophical functions

sensual colours flirt with elements of form
fighting off the influences of the norm
refining and beautifying with organic bliss
planting on the canvas an elegant kiss

throw the paint against the wall
go sing dirges in the hall
pull the covers round you ears
and wipe away your tears

Thirty-Seven

at the university the students studied books
and groomed their good looks
trying to impress
as they did undress

oh mother dear
may I drink beer
she said of course
you big old horse

a trick or two was known
a chance or two was blown
the stranger was unknown
a toad was turned to stone

three witches standing in a row
where the river stopped to flow
they counted to three and cast a spell
and thus invented hell

then they decided to throw the dice
and threw into the pot a pair of mice
with an abra ca dabra in the air
of unicorns they created a pair

a silly bit of frivolous fun
is just as good as a juicy bum
as clowns dance and act their part
and laugh the crazy world apart

the professor ranted on about invention
with a nod to proper and good convention
taking care to salute his peers
half of them being a bunch of queers

and even though it makes some sad
being queer is not half bad
it's what it is oh noble friend
there's nothing there to mend

why can't we just be nice
and make no one pay a price
for being who they are
accepting them on par

it's an evil potion that the witches sprinkle
as the natives stand around and tinkle
turning goblins into ghouls
and politicians into fools

permission granted to fly to the moon
hope to see you soon
and please change your socks
and bring back a few nice rocks

in outer space our home shall be
that's where we'll live you and me
among the stars so bright
we'll shine just like a light

Mother Earth to thee we pledge
as we stand upon this ledge
that we will always faithful be
and never kill a tree

mankind is the great polluter
creating mayhem on our computer
we've made a lot of junk
we're really in a funk

the black chair
flew through the air
what a sight
what a fright

Thirty-Eight

a man climbed into a bin
and made quite a din
to gather bottles and a platter
and about to clatter

the fornicator was forgiven
even as to the field he was driven
and there they took his life
as they stabbed him with a knife

the ancient customs are so cruel
making the rebels drink the gruel
making stupid demands
then cutting off their hands

justice laughs as she cries
as the prisoner dies
mankind is conflicted
and also convicted

for goodness sake
don't drive into the lake
instead learn to bake
a tasty little cake

once upon a time
there was a lovely rhyme
about a girl who danced a jig
with a lovely canadian pig

you may laugh
or plot a graph
or saw a broad in half
or pet a calf

or spray some ban
upon your tan
then crouch
as you say ouch

the bandaid covered the cut
that was on her butt
after she slipped and fell
into a well

she had smoked some dope
but they pulled her out with a rope
and now she's drinking wine
and feeling fine

do you think
if the pen runs out of ink
that you will disappear
is that your fear

and then reappear in another world
with your hair all curled
and your panties in a knot
is that what you thought

oh ye of little faith
so scared of outer space
oh dear
why do we fear

casting all our cares upon the crucified
we become holy and deified
with crosses in our hands
and our heads wrapped in elastic bands

march in order
off to the border
where we will buy stuff at the duty free
and have a good long pee

Thirty-Nine

I saw the bravery in the face of the brutality
a reinvention of civility
shield girl was her name
protesting evil was her game

the brutal dictatorships we must not tolerate
stop the hate
and open up the gate
and be democratic and great

for totalitarian regimes we have no room
all they bring is doom
and gloom
sweep it out with a democratic broom

all people should be free
it's the only way to be
our leaders stand in the way
as with the evil they trade and play

like MLK all people have a dream
and I hear them scream
can't you see
we should be free

in a cage the tigers prowl
in the office the secretaries scowl
the umpire calls foul
and in the pen the lions growl

locked up without committing a crime
laying there in all that grime
innocence betrayed
justice misplayed

how can it be
that we who are free
simply linger
and do not lift a finger

we must make the case
that freedom is for the entire human race
and make a choice
to lift our voice

from the mountains we will shout
together we have clout
and demand
freedom for their land

are we such cowards still
that we do not have the will
to be strong
and correct the wrong

in the Middle East they suffer
in China they have no buffer
in N.Korea they die
and in Viet Nam they cry

remember when the wall came down
it wiped away the frown
from the faces of the oppressed
they were no longer depressed

they drank freedom like a drink
all we heard was a giant clink
as all the way down to the coast
people drank a toast

we must use our might
to enforce the people's right
and stop the hypocrisy
preventing this democracy

Forty

the gangs of Harlem are tight
fearless they like to fight
on the internet they surf
in the streets they protect their turf

the streets are rough
but these guys are tough
the switchblades are ready
the nerves are steady

watch the eagle in the sky
as he soars way up high
the beauty of his flight
is such an incredible sight

America is a gangsters paradise
where everybody rolls the dice
trying to do the bee bop
and end up at the top

if you suck upon a soother
then you are a loser
and if you get a shiner
don't become a whiner

in the end
diamonds are a girls best friend
and if you want to be bold
get a lot of gold

money talks
bullshit walks
and it sucks to be a whore
and it sucks to be poor

and it ain't right
that the rich have all the might
we need to change the game
so everyone can live the same

in the shack
lived a guy named mack
he liked to drink his tea
and go outside to pee

all those pent-up ravings
to vocalize those supernatural cravings
find their way into our songs
as we visualize the models thongs

when the Saviour died
all the virgins cried
they crucified their king
the bells all stopped to ring

then the news was rife
that he had come back to life
and still we're left to wonder
was it all a blunder

and God is taking a lot of flack
cause Jesus hasn't been seen back
what's going on up there
does anyone even care

would God really dare
to produce an apocalyptic scare
and cause such an obstruction
with all the destruction

go tell it on the mountain
go and drink from the fountain
of life and never die
is that a lie

Forty-One

in fourteen ninety two
Columbus sailed the ocean blue
and then he ate some pizza
went home and painted the Mona Lisa

greatness is achievable
though not always believable
it's tempting to dare
to change the shape of a square

you can lie
but the laws of physics still apply
and you will see
you can't change gravity

it's a big deal
that we can fly on wings of steel
up and up we go
how far we just don't know

in this darkness we grope
fuelled by a thing called hope
a yearning to reach for the stars
as we drown our sorrows in our bars

we uncover
as we also discover
by curiosity inspired
our imagination fired

but there are those who love their meds
and remain as dreamers in their beds
preferring to complain and pout
never venturing to get out

they aspire to victimhood
being offended is what they think is good
poor me is what they say
they never see a sunny day

everything is bad
they are always sad
turning off the light
they don't like what's bright

all day long they criticize
and eat their pity pies
and it's sad they choose
to lose

greatness is for those who dare
to change the shape of a square
and not be bound by all the rules
we learned in all our loser schools

watch the mortician
as bound by tradition
he sprinkles dust upon the dead
and rubs his thoughtless head

out on the street sits the bum
his mind is tired and numb
he bids us all to come
and act a little dumb

throw a dollar in his cap
buy him clothes from the gap
celebrate his craziness
and indulge his laziness

why win when you can lose
it's what we sometimes choose
and isn't it a pity
that we become so bitty

Forty-Two

he was an English naturalist
a famous biologist
he led a revolution
with his concept of evolution

the fittest shall survive
the rest shall not revive
you must be fit
or feel like shit

and now we champion the weak
and pet them as they squeak
encouraging them to cry
and deeply sigh

the werewolves hide in the forest
with the rock and roll guitarist
trying to make a difference
by singing songs about deliverance

they belong to a spooky cult
in Satan they do exult
sacrificing chickens in the park
and doing voodoo after dark

their dreams are short and plump
they look for treasures in the dump
rubbing coins against the rocks
and wearing bright and holy socks

in a rubber tire they swing
offerings of shredded cheese they bring
chanting softly as they prance
all around the fire they dance

to the lord of hell they pray
swearing that they will obey
and serve their evil lord
as they sing in a minor chord

back in the train
where everyone is insane
and the conductor plays ginny
with a guy named vinny

the train is on its way to Rome
to an ecclesiastical dome
there secrets will be revealed
where once the blood conjealed

Saint Peter was crucified here
after he had a couple beer
and when he counted to seven
they sent him off to heaven

after him Saint Paul took over
when Jesus gave him the lucky clover
and gave him back his sight
after a terrible fright

and now we have the pope
who is nothing but a clueless dope
talking endless crap
he should go take a nap

it's no wonder that we're shaking
in our boots we are a-quaking
there's too much rust
in whom should we trust

the deities have run amuck
our own leader is a schmuck
it's a weird day
and no one knows the way

Forty-Three

you're not necessarily a fool
if you ain't cool
so why
do you even try

coolness is a state of mind
and you will find
that you ain't a fool
if you're not cool

just like it sounds like crap
when a white person tries to rap
it's not your thing
so learn to sing

the buzz in my ear
is what I hear
strange voices are talking
the ghosts are stalking

don't sneeze
pass the chocolates please
flick your bicks
I need a fix

dude walks into a gallery
it used to be a factory
and likes the paintings on the wall
he feels the call

come and worship in this cathedral of art
sit on the primordial cart
sing praises to artists everywhere
come and admire or just stare

she was a coffee drinker
he was a deep thought thinker
together they made history
it was a mystery

the lawyer made his point
as his client smoked a joint
then off to jail he went
his charm had all been spent

go to the thrift store and buy a chair
then go to the bathroom to comb your hair
it's so much fun
to get things done

I wonder if Cupid
is stupid
some of his arrows missed
and the people got pissed

in love so madly
then out so sadly
go mourn at the cliffs of Dover
and cry because it's over

play us a love song my dear
and pour us another beer
we're all verklempt
as the passion is spent

go and ask your mother
if you should look for another
how do you want to live
do you have love to give

maybe just eat some steak
and stay away from another heartbreak
protect yourself from pain
before you go insane

Forty-Four

it's eerie
and I'm so weary
just let me rest
and get undressed

the pace is far too fast
I wonder will I last
if someone would only bake
for me a lovely cake

why am I so cold
I think I'm getting old
what can I say
my hair is getting grey

I used to be so wired
and now I'm only tired
the doctor says I need some sun
and have a lot more fun

why was I so uncouth
when I was but a youth
now that I'm old I've much more class
and don't act like such an ass

it seems like such absurdity
that I've attained maturity
I miss the good old days
and all those bad boy ways

he said my dear
I feel the end is near
she replied give it a rest
you're making me depressed

the ball was smashed
the airplane crashed
where are the subscribers
when there are no survivors

no one wants a part of tradgedy
we run from adversity
as thoughts collide
and feelings hide

do a good deed
help me in my time of need
the grim reaper's at the door
I'm shaking to the core

it does no good to be crying
when you are dying
but it's what we do
to make it through

please make the monsters go away
I don't want them to stay
all those scary faces
are leaving evil traces

staring blankly into space
making a case
for losing one's apples
or snapples

even though you paid your dues
the doctor still gives you the bad news
oh what a fright
as you vow to fight

I let out a scream
as I wake up from this dream
what's in this air
I really had a scare

Forty-Five

no one got hurt
as the orchestra played emotionally at the concert
Brahms is always so inspiring
especially with the players so untiring

the conductor was delighted
to see his orchestra so united
their energy so high
it made him want to cry

he waved his baton furiously
as the audience looked on curiously
the strings were divine
and the french horn sublime

the timpani had a sound like thunder
you had to wonder
if the sky was falling
or was the lord himself calling

spiritual forces were connected to the instruments
and sweet was the dissonance
that the composer had commissioned
and the conductor envisioned

the mood was at once exquisite and dark
so moody and stark
with undertones of bohemian angst
and from the audience murmurs of thanks

the audience whispered as they left the auditorium
as if they were in a sanitarium
what a night of feeling
it was like a healing

rejuvenated and reborn
and a little bit forlorn
after a night of ethereal ecstasy
and longing fantasy

it was a trip to inner space
to showcase
a psychological interpretation of artistic flair
going where few would dare

pulling back the curtain of our estrangement
exposing the forces of our derangement
and highlighting our natural isolation
which causes our vexation

in this tension we ponder
as we wander
getting lost in our own worlds of wonder
as Brahm's music tears us asunder

leaving us speechless
and breathless
and searching for traces
among the hidden places

inside the performance has left us shaken
as we slowly awaken
to a transcendental illumination
which can be our salvation

and bring us back to the garden
there to strike a bargain
to bring our souls back into realignment
and end our sad confinement

the cold air hits our faces
as we leave the special spaces
energized and uplifted
our focus shifted

Forty-Six

wham bam thank you mam
let's get together and make scme jam
and spread it on some bread
then go to bed

and snore the night away
ready to face a new day
baby put on your game face
and dream of outer space

it's all the same
as we strive for fame
and save our money
so we can love our honey

and breed
observing the latest creed
and if we're not barren
raising our children

it is our purpose in life to propogate
and then to assimilate
to be strong
to be as one

we can be so base
this human race
wasting so much time on hatred
instead of on the sacred

why are we so set on destroying
all that we find annoying
can we not learn
for peace to deeply yearn

sisters and brothers
fathers and mothers
all interwoven in a tapestry
of interconnected ancestry

when will we see our liberation
from the shackles of discrimination
and banish prejudice
and all malice

it seems to be addictive
to be vindictive
as cruelly begets further abuse
for which there is no excuse

the competition was intense
as the horses jumped over another fence
all trying to win the race
and come in first place

it's not only in the west
that we want to be the best
we struggle against inferiority
to attain superiority

what team ever plays to lose
it's not what we choose
is it a sin
to win

survival of the fittest
means the dying of the sickest
which goes against our moral progress
a diabolical game of chess

we need to heal the sick and cure the lame
and do it all in Jesus name
he showed the way
to a brand new day

Forty-Seven

shiny and new
pretty and blue
strong and tough
brazen and rough

we know it
we want it
we like it
we adore it

watch them sparkle see them shine
diamonds they are so very fine
they stand for status and for fame
big time players in the game

John may have a tiny weenie
but he drives a Lamborghini
Freddy may be insignificant and small
but with a Porsche he stands real tall

money is the compensator
and becomes the dominator
allowing for efficiencies
over physical deficiencies

she was a hedonistic free spirit living
out her fantasies and giving
much of herself to selfish souls
who loved to fill the holes

living out life in an orgy of excess
is not a life that God will bless
and I would guess
that few could deal with all the stress

he was a wimp
who loved his shrimp
he spat on sidewalks
and went for long walks

when he was not stinking
he was thinking
and when he was not walking
he was talking

he was a serious man
who loved to plan
how he would teach and school
a world that he would rule

dear Adolph why
did so many have to cry
or sigh
or die

the brutality of unrestrained egos
is something that goes
against our human values
it's bad news

have we learned from all the mistakes
we must put on the brakes
and stop idolizing vain and evil men
who want to lock us in a pen

the martyrs cry out from the ghettos
as ruby prances about in her stilettos
her shadow falling on the poor
who pay her to be a whore

in the shanty towns the people suffer
as walls are built to provide a buffer
so the rich can live in peace
and stop the poor from getting a piece

Forty-Eight

I wonder if we could
would we change our childhood
or our neighborhood
I wonder if we would

on the merrygoround we go
putting on a show
how fast will we spin
everybody in

we buy our candy at the corner store
and always want more
rotten teeth is what we get
but we're not dead yet

doing homework was no fun
we'd rather play and run
we learned a lot at all the schools
and still remained a bunch of fools

at least we know how to write and read
and recite some kind of creed
we memorized a lot of crap
and sometimes got the strap

then there was little Sammy Horner
always standing in the corner
for misbehaving and chewing gum
that kid was dumb

and Ilse she was smart
but what a tart
bringing apples to the teacher
and blow jobs for the preacher

the cool guys had cars
and snuck into the bars
with older chicks
they were such dicks

time hurries on by
as we eat some pumpkin pie
and listen to old hits
as our own kids have fits

I don't know if it pays
to think about the good old days
it just makes me sad
and I miss my dad

with the curtain falling
the future is calling
and so we make new plans
to get new fans

who is going to like us now
where are we going to go to get some chow
chew on oh oldie
let's find a goldie

at least there's no more books
now we love the cooks
and we love to eat
as we dance to the old beat

some got tired of being fools
and so went back to the schools
to learn about computers
and ride about in scooters

all of us young or old
would love to find a pot of gold
to satisfy the itch
of wanting to get rich

Forty-Nine

gravity is the manifestation of the ether vacuum
syndrome
as elections roam
and create electronic vacuums
without fumes

and so all masses suck at each other
as they smother
exerting force
to change the course

Einstein had a lot to say
in his good old day
and the old boys
don't want to play with new toys

and so they disregard
the avantegarde
which has new ideas
about the Koreas

and about atoms and the role
they play in our soul
and also in gravity
and levity

our nostalgia should not be a detraction
from understanding the forces of attraction
rethinking theories from the past
should be a blast

it's a folly
to be so melancholy
and eat old cream
instead of daring to dream

out of the twentieth century we must crawl
and quit playing with Einsteins doll
heed the call
and get on the ball

there is no such thing as spacetime
might as well suck on a lime
and for the fabric of space
there isn't a case

we drown in our nonsense
why are we so very dense
as if instead of brains
we have a bunch of drains

when you build on false assumptions
with silly old presumptions
it's all just fuddle duddle
and you swim in a puddle

try your powers of persuasion
with an abstract mathematical equation
where this equals that
and you see a black cat

Einstein had an abstract notion
about celestial motion
as he indulged in fantasy
whilst smoking pot on his balcony

I think it's sad
that he went mad
and tried to solve the riddle
with all his piddle

the earth revolves around the sun
a lot of fun
but I still cry
why

Fifty

they say there is no deity
then how did we come to be
and how did it get started
was it that someone just farted

out of a pool of chemicals life was created
that's what the experts stated
bam
ka zam

give your head a shake
and go and bake
a lovely cake
that's what you should make

it's all very mysterious
and so serious
when we talk about the origin of life
and all that strife

do we really exist
shapes in the mist
maybe only shadows
who knows

I threw a ball up in the air
I didn't care
that I was bare
and caused a scare

it came back
and I got a wack
on my head
which sent me to bed

where I stayed for days and days
and finally repented of all my evil ways
when I doubted that God existed
oh how I was twisted

what was I thinking
why was I stinking
up the place
by being a basket case

accept what the elders preach
swallow what the teachers teach
and never ask
about what they try to mask

with theoretical bits of shit
that make you look like a twit
even as you are sly
and catch them in a lie

they saddle us with their theories
and it worries
those of us who question their truth
and feel that it's uncouth

the demonstrations of spirituality
are considered banality
and therein lies their folly
and their source of melancholy

we sail on the gospel ship
and try to get a grip
and a sense of what's going on
without falling prey to a con

it's so grand
our beautiful land
give me your hand
and together we will stand